Triplets! Seriously?!!

'Ant'ics of the Topsy Tiddlers

Rheanna Mouktika Kantipudi

BlueRose ONE.com
Stories Matter
NewDelhi • London

BLUEROSE PUBLISHERS
India | U.K.

For permissions requests or inquiries regarding this publication, please contact:

BLUEROSE PUBLISHERS
www.BlueRoseONE.com
info@bluerosepublishers.com
+91 8882 898 898
+4407342408967

ISBN: 978-93-5819-578-1

Cover Design: Muskan Sachdeva & Ruchira Carolyn Kantipudi
Illustrated By: Himanshi Joshi & Ruchira Carolyn Kantipudi
Typesetting: Pooja Sharma

First Edition: June 2024

To my beautiful sister Ruchira Carolyn ... my first and best friend.

Contents

JUNGLE

HeHe..........

The Triplets

Three little ants,

Lived far away,

Down in the jungle,

And up the grassy lane.

Of a great family of nine,

They are the last three born,

Not exactly the peaceful kind,

That you will sooner or later find.

Their names are Ruby, Emerald, and Sapphire Falls,

All jewels-precious to their mother they are

But most definitely the naughtiest ones of all.

If candy is missing, or a pie or two,

You'll catch them running with them away from you!

Pocket money goes on ice cream,
Their excelling point is making people scream,
The adventures they've been in,
And the troubles too,
All because of a slight deed of mischief,
When you've read them all, you'll say phew!

But under that troublesome curtain,
Lie three hearts bigger than anyone for certain,
For putting their behaviour aside,
They are the most fun-loving and kind!

Chapter 1

Welcome to the World, Triplets!

It was a chilly weekend morning in the Ant household with the aroma of warm banana pancakes still wafting through the large house. Everyone slowly settled into their usual holiday routines when they heard a scream from the nursery.

"Oh, Mom, Dad, Angel Falls! Come soon! Something's happening in the egg basket," shrieked Niagara Falls, completely beside herself in horror, " Have I tripped over them by mistake?"

A very alarmed Mrs. Ant ran over from the kitchen to see what the fuss was about, why her dearest daughter was in a panic. Her eldest daughter Angel Falls sprinted from her desk too while Mr. Ant lazed on the couch with his newspaper, presuming his dramatic little daughter was overreacting to something as usual. Pink and Orange Falls, the youngest girl twins couldn't be bothered to join in the family confusion as they had just gotten their noses into encyclopedias 6 & 8; the new ones they just got for their birthday.

Oddly enough, the little triplet ants seemed to be hatching- way... way before they were expected at Christmas. Out popped a tiny face each, approximately one a minute out of the ruby, sapphire and emerald-coloured little eggs that Niagara Falls had insisted on painting - just so they would look 'colourful'. Well, the Ant family couldn't have foreseen in a million years just how much colour they would add to their lives.

"We're hungry, something smells nice, who are you?", they asked a bamboozled Mrs. Ant who was absolutely convinced she was seeing things.

Finishing up food in the egg so quickly and hatching famished was unheard of in the jungle they lived in. All of her older children had more or less been on time- with Angel Falls on the more and Niagara on the less - and Pink and Orange Falls on the dot (Goldilocks timing); here were her little triplets making history in the ant colony - a trait that soon became a trademark or rather hallmark of her little ones.

Mr. Ant nearly had a heart attack! "Call whom?" he asked.

"The ambulance of course dear, we've got to get the triplets checked to make sure everything is alright ," answered Mrs. Ant, frantically rummaging for their tiddly car's keys.

"We're just hungry Mom, we're fine," they whined, "Can we eat before we go?"

Everything whirled into a blur as the paramedics strapped the triplets into tiny stretchers and whisked the whole family away as everyone looked like they needed to go to the hospital for an emergency check-up. Pronto!

ER received with trepidation the chalk-white faced Falls family with the exception of the enthusiastic triplets gaily waving past everyone with a 'Hiya folks!'

As staff attended to the rest of the family, Mrs. Ant recovered barely enough to recount the details of the unexpected unceremonious arrival of the triplets and begged the paediatrician to double-check or rather triple- check the new born infants to assess their viability in the world at that young age. He laughingly assured her that he could see nothing wrong but if she insisted he would keep them in for a few days of observation. The triplets were accommodated in the baby animal nursery where they miraculously fell asleep after a massive feed.

"Excuse me, excuse me, oops! Excuse me!" chanted the triplets, as they made their way out of the nursery to the nurses' station, stepping on a pair of adorable lion cubs, baby elephants, kittens and a baby blue whale who were all fast asleep. "Do you have any treats for us?" they asked the astonished nurses on duty.

Needless to say, the pint- sized triplets were slated to be the most peculiar ones the jungle hospital had ever welcomed!

Chapter 2

The Triplets Show Themselves Around

The Ant home was now inhabited by three new additions to the Falls family who had proved to be anything but peaceful. Mr. and Mrs. Ant's room welcomed three coloured cradles placed lovingly beside their mother.

True to their quite new names, the Triplets had adopted the colour sense that matched their names and would refuse to have anything to do with another colour; which meant that everything belonging to them had to be 'jewel-coloured', as they referred to it.

The Triplets settled quite quickly into their new surroundings and rapidly became familiar with their new family members. The doting, calm eldest sister Angel Falls was a little astonished at their speaking abilities at such a young age, but eventually got used to them. Rather talkative, hyper, straight-forward and blunt Niagara Falls readily accepted them into the family as they 'livened things up a bit' as she reckoned.

The former youngest of the lot, the twins Pink and Orange Falls did not mind their rambunctious triplet sisters but preferred the relevant silence in the study and their ever-present encyclopedias. On the whole, the children were all fairly comfortable with the new kids on the block and soon got used to the fact that they were rather far from normal, regular ants.

But two ants of the family had still not recovered from the shock of their recent past. One was Mrs. Ant. Ever since they had returned home from the hospital she was very concerned about how they would behave at home and was still trying to grasp the absurdity of the last two weeks. Another was, of course, Mr. Ant, who as the placid-to-a-point kind of father had never experienced anything such as this in his easy-going life and was continuing to struggle with the task of explaining to his friends and colleagues how unsettling the whole process was. Yes, getting used to the Triplets was going to be quite a tall order.

Being babies, the Triplet's daily routine was rather monotonous, consisting of sleeping, going to the bathroom, eating (the most crucial one) and sleeping again and this didn't sit very well with them.

"Ruby!" whispered Sapphire Falls one afternoon as she rolled to one side in her cradle, "Are you awake?"

" Of course, I am," came the toneless reply, "I'm so bored of sleeping in this cradle for hours and hours!"

" So, am I," replied Sapphire," Do you have any ideas on what to do? I think Mum's having a nap, so are all our sisters and Dad's at work."

"Hmm...," thought Ruby, and when the Triplets start thinking something surely happens, " In that case, why don't we explore the house for a bit?"

"Ooh! That'll be exciting!" exclaimed Sapphire, "We haven't actually seen this house much, apart from the bedroom and bathroom which I'm tired of seeing!"

"Alright then", Ruby said, taking full charge as the oldest one, "Wake up Emerald, she's still sleeping and let's go troops!" Poor Emerald Falls was woken up and informed about the just-made decision. As the youngest one, she was a little more relaxed than the others, but nonetheless shared their excitement and mischievous nature.

The great exploration of the house first had to start with the journey to the floor from their cradles.

"It's a long way down there..." stuttered Emerald, peering down the edge of her cradle at the mosaic tiles, "And we've only just learnt to walk." she realised uncomfortably.

"Oh, no matter!", said Ruby, confidently, "Just climb down these rods!

Needless to say, it was much easier said than done, but finally, their tiny little feet precariously landed on the ground.

"That's a relief!" they said as they made their way out of the bedroom as quietly as church mice or should we say ants? Their little feet pattered up the corridor and suddenly halted as they noticed a door wide open into a room.

"Hey," said Sapphire, "Have a look at this!"

They gazed in awe at all the library books, enormous desks and chairs that were so tall to them they would have reached the clouds. The room was painted in a soft light blue much to Sapphire's evident delight.

"Come on," said Ruby hastily, "there's a lot more to explore!"

They walked into a large sunny room with comfy white sofas, a big screen television and paintings of flowers that adorned the lemon-yellow walls. It was the living room.

"These look really comfy," said Emerald, as she climbed one of the sofas.

"And bouncy too!" laughed Sapphire, as she jumped up and down on them.

And soon, all three of them were bouncing high on the sofa, sending the big orange cushions flying all over the place without even a thought of what their parents would have to say to them. After they had jumped to their heart's content, they explored other corners of the large room.

"Ooh!" squealed Ruby, "I can see myself in this!"

She pointed to a dark rectangular shape on the wall and soon enough, they were all standing in front of the TV doing silly dance moves and admiring themselves. But, of course, nothing could hold their interest for long and soon enough they marched out of the living room, in a line to their next destination.

"Now this is a funny one," they thought, as they thoroughly examined the room they ended up in.

It had many wooden-squared cabinets all along one side of the room and a long stretch of gleaming counters. Attached to the centre wall was a humongous box with push buttons and dials on the front of it.

"Woah!" exclaimed the triplets as they looked up around the room.

"I wonder what's inside these funny-looking doors" pondered Sapphire Falls aloud as she advanced towards a very interesting-looking cupboard.

"Let's check it out!" encouraged Ruby Falls.

But to their dismay, the knob was far too high for them to reach.

"Oh!" sighed Emerald, after trying several times to reach the handle.

"Maybe we need something to help reach there," said Ruby thoughtfully, "Like a step or something that helps us go higher!"

"That's an idea", commented Emerald, "But where are we going to get something like that?

"There!" shrieked Sapphire as she pointed towards a little stepladder in the corner.

With that, the triplets raced towards the ladder and with all their might, pushed it towards the cupboard.

"Pheew!" said Sapphire, once they were done, "Now let's climb up and look around."

They all at once tried to climb and unexpectedly were successful in their attempt.

"Yes! We made it!" they yelled, clapping their feelers together excitedly.

They started to open the handle and it swung open easily. It was filled with tins of cake and biscuits and other goodies but since it was all food, they didn't really care what it was. They squealed in delight and dived into their kind of goodness!

"This is the life!" exclaimed Sapphire. "You betcha!" the others agreed.

But as the triplets were blissfully unaware and in biscuit haven, Mrs. Ant had just woken up and was shocked to find empty cradles beside her bed. She hastily drew her slippers on and ran out of the room. The sound of footsteps echoed through the house, heard by everyone but the triplets. Mrs. Ant looked in all the rooms for them and was appalled at the state of the sofa, but continued her search. She didn't have to look for long because just as she stepped into the kitchen, she spotted them crunching up chocolate cream cookies and whatnot!

"Triplets!" she hollered, aghast at the sight of the crumb-covered triplets.

"Oh ha-ha," chuckled the triplets nervously, "Hi Mum, did you have a nice nap?"

"Really, what has come over you?" she gasped in bewilderment, "Now get out of the cupboard this instant!"

"Yes, Mummy" they whined as they brushed themselves off and went to the cradles, their mum wondering whether the luxury of naps would be too much to ask with the Triplets' prodigious personalities.

Once they were all tucked into bed, they boarded the train to Dreamland faster than any bullet train. Sweet dreams were not exactly the kind they had that day, but at least they learnt to always listen and obey their mother for their own safety!

Chapter 3

Meeting the Red Ant Triplets

The Triplets were now growing up fast and were old enough to play simple games and hang out with their older sisters.

They found out soon enough, that their best bet was being around their oldest sister Angel Falls. She simply adored the trio to bits and was always ready to cuddle and play with them. She ignored many of their impish qualities and focused solely on their cuteness factors, which they just loved.

It wasn't so easy to wrap wool around Niagara Falls' eyes though. As much as they loved her sparky personality (quite like theirs) they weren't too keen on the firm hand she kept on them.

Pink and Orange were nice to talk to for a while, but then they would go on about something rather interesting in their encyclopedias which didn't particularly interest the Triplets. All in all, they enjoyed life to the max! But their social interaction, interestingly enough, didn't stop there, much to their own surprise.

One particularly bitterly cold morning, the Triplets were in a huddle up on the sofa, fixing a puzzle or at least trying to fix one. The rest of the family lazed around on the other grey fabric sofas and read. Suddenly, the telephone rang and Niagara dashed off to answer it. She came back almost instantly, with a big grin plastered on her wide face.

"That was Aunty Red Ant," she said happily, the grin extending even more, "She says she's super excited that she can finally come to see the Triplets and will be here today by noon."

The rest of the family cheered with approval but Mr. Ant looked startled.

"Today!" he spluttered as he was just enjoying his tea, "But we aren't in the mood or shape for any company! He obviously spoke for himself as the rest of the family clapped their hands in excitement.

"Calm down," said Mrs. Ant soothingly, "Well just tell them to meet us at a restaurant and then come home."

As Mr. and Mrs. Ant discussed the details thoroughly, The Triplets asked the Twins in a whisper , "Wait, who is this Aunty Red Ant?"

" Oh, Aunty Red Ant is the funniest, most wonderful aunt in the world!" they replied, "She always brings the best candy and of course will bring her triplets along and Uncle Red Ant!"

"Her Triplets!" The Triplets gave her a quizzical stare, "We thought We were one of a kind, one in a million Triplets!"

"Uh...no" said the Twins, giving them the didn't-you-know side eye, "Those triplets were born a month before you all"

"Ooh!" gasped the Triplets, "wonder what they're like..."

"Your menu, Madame" proffered the butler as they were seated at a huge table reserved in a secluded alcove. They had all just trooped into the humongous restaurant gaping at the glistening chandeliers, and stylish cream and gold tables with matching dishes and silverware all in apple-pie order. Although usually, food was the most prominent on their radar, today they were beside themselves with curiosity about these new Triplets they were to meet. A wonder list: Would they be just like them? Would they also share their love for anything edible?

As the Triplets craned their necks to spot them, soon enough a family of red ants walked through the sliding doors. They seemed a bit too red, almost like a line of cherry tomatoes. Smartly outfitted in ivory frocks, coats and shoes, they were a picture of everything prim and proper. Their feelers neatly held in satin ribbons bobbed up and down as they nodded most politely at everything said at the table. They looked rather nice but before the Triplets could think anything more, Aunty Red Ant simply flung herself on them in a cascade of hugs and kisses. The look of horror on their faces was so evident that everyone seated at the table was finding it hard to stifle their laughter.

After Aunty Red Aunt was finished with them, she proceeded to commence the hugging ceremony with every other sibling at the table.

Right behind her were the pristine Red Ant Triplets who stared in wonder at the Triplets who looked a bit ridiculous in their jewel-coloured frocks, ribbons already half undone. The Red Ant Triplets, first put their hands out gingerly saying "How do you do?" After that initial unease, the ice began to melt as they chattered happily.

" So, what do you like to do for fun?" asked the Triplets gaily, "Oh, we are avid readers," replied the Red Ant Triplets, "and do book reviews for our friends. We also run the quiz and crossword fun club in the neighbourhood."

"Oh!" said the Triplets, not understanding how anything like that could possibly be fun, "Well err..., we like to eat and play - though sometimes that causes trouble!

"What sort of trouble?" asked the Red Ants, puzzled in turn at the choice of such trivial pursuits in life.

"Oh, trouble with Mummy for sneaking into the snacks and stuff and maybe some trouble with the people in the hospital too," they said, scratching their heads as they tried hard to remember the millions of episodes of havoc they had already wreaked.

"We've never really experienced much trouble so far," said the Red Ant Triplets, looking as if it were a completely foreign concept.

The Triplets looked up in surprise.

As the polite chit-chat continued, they began to feel rather bored with these new cousins of theirs. Aunty Red Ant was a totally different story of course, as she took the lead of the conversation at the table. "No wonder Uncle Red Ant was so quiet," thought the Triplets to themselves. Finally, they got so tired of them that they thought that it would be a good idea to get a good look around this new place. They slowly slipped under the table, no one noticing them gone. They jumped in glee! This was going to be fun!

They sauntered off to the reception desk and gazed in awe at the large reservation books and the fancy decor dotting the area. But the thing that caught their attention the most was the large designer telephone that sat, gleaming on the lowest level of the desk. They were having a fine time crawling all around it and sitting on it until the phone gave a shrill ring that echoed through the restaurant. The Triplets who were sitting on it gave a yell of surprise but assumed nobody had heard it as it seemed peaceful enough. The phone kept ringing and at last, the Triplets picked it up.

"Allo?" said the voice on the phone.

"Hello!" they replied, most courteously.

"Have you thought about zee merger of my French patisserie vit yours?"

"Wow, French pastries sound fine Mister!" they said, pleased.

"All right zen, I will sign zee papers and meet you today to dizcuss zee detailz! Au revoir!" farewelled the mystery voice with the thick European accent. "Au...what?" questioned the Triplets, but the phone had just been hung up with a click.

"That's nice," said Ruby, "Now, we'll have French macaroons for dessert if they're ever going to bring them!"

"Yay!" they exclaimed as they leapt for a tri-five!

"Now let's go before anyone sees we're gone," said Emerald, as they scurried out of there. But the Triplets were quite wrong there! Someone had seen them go! And that someone or should say somebodies were... The Red Ant Triplets! After a minute or two, they noticed the Triplets' disappearance and decided to follow them. They were right behind the counter when the Triplets answered the call. Now that the Triplets were leaving they also thought they would leave slowly.

Just as they were crawling out, a man, clad in a black hoodie and jeans, stole through the revolving doors to the reception desk, stealthily pocketing all the money from the cash drawer. Someone screamed and everybody was definitely in a tizzy running helter-skelter in all directions. As for the Triplets, they were just on the way back to their table and heard the noise and hid under a chair, just next to the thief most unfortunately.

The Red Ant Triplets were still on the shelf, trembling in their boots as the thug shot a bullet up to the roof to silence the crowd. Suddenly out of nowhere, a big burly cop came up right behind him and caught him easily by the neck. Everyone in the restaurant clapped and cheered but what nobody had noticed were the Triplets cowering in fright under the chair. Just then the officer shoved the chair away, not noticing the Triplets and was about to pin the thief to the ground so he could handcuff him.

The Red Ant Triplets saw this and almost instantly leapt off the shelf like a trio of cheetahs and landed down near the chair and with the force of their landing pushed the Triplets away from being crushed under the weight of the man.

Mrs. Ant watched this scene in terror, paralyzed by the stress of the whole incident. Both Ant families gathered around the Triplets of both kinds frantically checking if they were okay.

"Triplets!" screamed their mum, anxiously.

"We're fine Mummy," they replied, "If it weren't for the Red Ant Triplets, we would be ant soup by now!"

"Oh, don't say such things!" said Mrs. Ant, breathlessly, wiping her forehead, "Never ever leave me when we're outside, is that understood?"

"Yes Mummy" they replied meekly.

The Red Ant Triplets, however, were the heroines of the hour and were being congratulated and thumped on the backs by everyone. The Triplets got up and gave them a big bear hug and kiss and a bunch of 'thank yous'. The Red Ant Triplets remained calm and composed and replied to all the compliments, "It was a reaction any ant faced with that kind of situation would carry out." Even the restaurant management and staff heartily congratulated them.

Just as the whole party of people were leaving the restaurant with Mr. and Mrs. Ant hoping nothing else would happen for the next month or so with the Triplets, a rather peculiar-looking man in a beret and duffle coat came up to the restaurant and asked, "Where is zee manager? I haf come to zpeak vit him today." They directed him to the manager and all the Triplets could say was 'Oh No!' and the Ant family understood what that meant when the manager threatened all sorts of punishments for the Triplets while on their way to the car.

But by then, they had already dozed off, dreaming about restaurants, French accents and all. Thank goodness the Red Ant Triplets were at their rescue when the thief broke in, otherwise, the Triplets would have encountered real danger. They learnt to always be by the side of their parents outdoors; a lesson they wouldn't forget in a hurry!

Chapter 4

The Triplets First Getaway

"Are we there yet?" asked the Triplets.

" No, we're not!" cried the Ant family for the hundredth time that day.

They were going to a summer cabin up on the hill set in beautiful wild flowers with a winding, pretty garden path that led to it. Everything about it was wonderful… except for the trip. But finally, they reached the house and as they were getting out of the car, they were greeted with a shrill whistle and the chug-chug of engines.

"What is that?" yelled the Triplets, hanging on to their mother's summer dress for dear life!

"Oh Triplets, don't be scared, it's only a train in a railway station ," she explained.

"Hmm… thought Mr Ant to himself, "I hope we can sleep well with that noise at night.", as he was rather piqued that Holiday homes.com conveniently avoided mention of such seemingly trivial information.

But what was going on in the Triplets' minds was quite different: "Wow! A railway station! Isn't that like the toy train ride that Mummy takes us to in the amusement park?"

They all trooped inside the house and made their way to the bedrooms.

"Let's unpack first and then eat," suggested Mrs. Ant. And they began throwing books, clothes, toys and what-not, all topsy-turvy on the bed.

Dinner and a couple of rounds of UNO later, night fell, and without the need of counting sheep, they were all asleep almost instantly, tired from all the excitement.

The next morning, the Triplets awoke first, disturbed from their peaceful slumber by a couple of curious cows poking their heads into their open windows. They dressed in their jewel-coloured playsuits and tumbled downstairs to find a silent, empty kitchen. Rather disgruntled at the sight of zero food when they entered the kitchen, they proceeded to sit at the dining table and wait somewhat patiently. Suddenly, they remembered something... the big toy train ride!

"Hey, why don't we hop across the fence to the station?" proposed Emerald, putting into words the feelings of the others.

And with that, they raced out of the house and set off towards the station. The station itself was right opposite their holiday home and took them no time at all to find it as the morning train's whistle was enough direction. They were having such a fun time in there, playing pirates that they didn't realise that the train was slowly pulling away.

"Got you, Buccaneer!" hollered Ruby Falls as she ran around the first-class compartment catching Sapphire Falls.

Just then, they heard a loud, monotone voice throughout the train. "Train to Springfield, stops at Hippo Hole, Mole Mountain and The Railway." droned the voice, as the Triplets halted to terror.

"Hey", stammered Ruby Falls, astonished, as she slightly jolted. "I don't think this is a ride! We're leaving the station!"

"Oh dear!", wailed the Triplets and scuttled to the front of the train. They ran straight into the driver's compartment and startled his assistant.

"Hey, kids!" he yelled, "Where are you running off to?"

"Oh, Mr. Driver, we're not supposed to be here!" said the Triplets in unison.

"What do you mean?" said the driver, Perks, putting his bald head around the compartment divider. So out came the story of everything and they began crying puddles of tears as huge as the Amazon river!

"Well, we can always get you home, you know afterwards" he commented, after listening intently to their entire story, as he pulled out a packet of chocolate biscuits. "Are you hungry?" he asked, grinning, not expecting the overenthusiastic reaction from the distressed trio.

And he was absolutely accurate, the triplets gobbled it up before you could say, Jack Robinson.

"Lookie here", showed Perks, pointing to an enormous noir handle sitting on the front control panel, "This lever makes the train go faster and this one slower"

"Oh!" exclaimed the Trips.

"And this one stops it, ain't that cool?" he explained, glancing down briefly to bend to their eye level.

"It is!" agreed the Triplets aghast at the number of buttons, cranks and levers.

For the rest of the journey, they chatted with Perks about all sorts of things. They found out that Perks had a family of three children. They also came to know he had a birthday coming up soon, but no one knew or sent him any presents. Taking a shortcut to drop the unintended voyagers home safely, the train pulled into their station and they said goodbye to Perks saying they would surely send him a present on his birthday.

"Bye mates," he said, waving his stubby hand jovially. "Don't you get lost on any other trains, alright?" he instructed sternly, with a bright twinkle in his eyes, thinking that it was adorable of them to think of sending him a gift.

"Alright!" chuckled the Triplets and rushed onto the platform waving madly.

They scurried back home only to find everyone still asleep. They too reckoned that it would be a good idea to catch a second round of forty winks and so duly tucked themselves in once again.

Once they woke up, Mrs. Ant called the Triplets, "Tripsies! Do you want to visit the railway station today after breakfast?"

"No thanks, Mom!" answered the Triplets, as they giggled, wincing uncomfortably on their recent escapade.

A few days later, Perks found a parcel in the post and undid the wrapping which revealed a gold watch studded with white shimmering stones around the dial. He gaped in amazement, as his fingers fumbled to open the floral hand-written card that accompanied it. 'Happy Birthday Perks!' read the note, with three squiggly signatures dotting the end of it. He smiled in gratitude, thinking to himself, how such small children could have made him so overjoyed on his birthday.

Back at the Ant Holiday Home, Mr Ant awoke cheerfully, awaiting a sumptuous breakfast. As he donned his new summer motley tee-shirt paired with some electric green shorts, he was having a rare 'I-love-my-life' moment, staring into the mirror at his reflection. But his admiring reverie was broken by the jarring sound of his phone's ringtone. The caller introduced himself as the local stationmaster, who was enquiring about the cute kids who travelled Route 64 a couple of days ago. As the call progressed, his face became redder and redder as he was informed about the morning's happenings. As he put down the phone, he sighed, nodding his head in frustration. He flung open the bedroom door and screeched "Triplets!!! " The Triplets dropped their teaspoons in fright at the dining table and turned to each other, "Oops!" they muttered, as they scuttled away to elucidate the whole nine yards of the story.

As wonderful as it may be, they were lucky that the driver was a jolly good fellow, but they learnt never to venture outside unbeknownst to their parents, as it could lead them into some pretty pickles!

Chapter 5

Mr. Lion's Listening Party

Life in the jungle was going rather well for the Triplets. Except for a few hiccups here and there, they were enjoying getting to know everyone around the Jungle and made friends big and small. Everything was going as smooth as butter, until one day something extraordinary happened to a very reputed member of the Jungle society, Mr. Lion.

It all started one rainy morning in the Lion household. Mrs. Lion was bustling around their spacious den kitchen and the cubs, Mona and Max were brushing their teeth vigorously, eager for a good meal of egg and cress sandwiches.

"Breakfast family!" called Mrs. Lion, setting plates out on the big dining table.

"Coming Mummy!" cried the cubs as they raced to the table and sat their furry little selves down. Mrs. Lion sat down and looked around at the table.

"Where's Daddy?" she asked, putting her fork down.

She got up and walked to the living room, only to find Mr. Lion in front of their television set, engrossed in a TV programme. She peered at the screen and saw a lion singing melodiously.

"Ahem, Lionel..." she started, "Oh hi!" said Mr. Lion turning around and looking rather surprised.

"Your breakfast is getting cold," she said, thinking about what could be keeping him so long.

"I was just watching this lion sing and I thought to myself, 'Don't I sing better than this?' I mean he's making a career out of this and he isn't even half as good as I am!" he rushed, striking a rather theatrical pose as if to prove his point.

He was just saved a scolding as the cubs came into the room wondering what was happening.

"Hey cubs!" called Mr. Lion.

"Yes Dad" they replied, simultaneously.

"Isn't this lion on TV cool?" he questioned expectantly, his furry face even more eager than it usually was.

"I guess ," said Mona, squinting at the screen.

"Did you know that your Daddy sings at least three times better?" he bragged, puffing his chest out and slicking his mane back, to reinforce the effect.

"But Daddy," began Max, "We've never even heard you sing!"

Mona and her mum tried hard to smother giggles.

"Oh well," said Mr Lion, trying to regain dignity, "I'll practise and show you what I can do!"

They all headed back to the table and ate quietly wondering what their eccentric father was up to next.

The next few weeks for Mr. Lion were extremely hectic . First, he rang up his old pal, Mr. Pink Panther whom he knew owned a recording studio. He was duly given a time slot to sing and record there, with a slight word of caution though, from Mr Pink Panther, to handle the equipment with care.

After recording a couple of songs there, he decided he ought to tell his friends about his new passion. He radiated joy as he rang up all the other jungle dads. Personally, Mr. Ant thought he had gone bonkers as usual; Mr. Blue Whale presumed that a bit of catnip was dropped into his meal at the office cafeteria and Mr. Cat gathered it as 'one of his Mr. Lion's crazy moods again'. Overall, the feedback wasn't what you'd call thrilling but it was enough for Mr. Lion. After a few weeks of recording and loads of discussions on the subject, he decided to hold a party for all the children of the Jungle, to showcase his brand-new talent.

Mrs. Lion scurried around with invitations to all the Jungle Children. Firstly, she popped around next door to the Very Pretty Kittens, Rosie and Posie, two cutesy big-eyed kittens, who lived in Cat Tower with their doting parents. Next, she trotted to the field just opposite to their den, to deliver invites to Ellie and Chellie Elephant, the Mayor's kids, two roly-poly baby elephants who loved playing day and night in the grasslands around the cul-de-sac.

She rummaged in her purse for the next one, which was addressed to the Bears; two caramel cubs who spent rather sweet days in their mother's bakery, tasting every honey cake they could find. Lastly, she wended her way to the edge of the Jungle where the ocean met the land, to invite Baby Blue Whale, a chubby little thing who was just learning how to swim without bumping into coral in the turquoise waters.

"A party!" squealed the Triplets, as Mrs. Ant finished her chat with Mrs. Lion outside their gate.

"Yes," said Mrs. Ant beaming at them, "And you can wear your new yellow frilly dresses!"

"But they're not jewel-coloured!" they protested, but it was like arguing with a brick wall as that's what their mom dressed them in after all.

"Hi Mona, hey Max!" called all the jungle kids as they trooped in through the back gate: Baby Blue Whale, the Very Pretty Kitties, Ellie and Chellie Elephants, the bear cubs, Peanut and Butter and of course, The Triplets, Pink and Orange Falls, Niagara Falls and Angel Falls.

"Hey everyone!" cried the cubs as they ushered their friends to the backyard where Mr. Lion was setting up his stage. The kids' jaws dropped ten feet when they saw a glowing Mr. Lion climb the stage aka back porch, all decked up in a golden jacket studded with shining sequins, a shirt with a rather over-starched collar also adorned with tiny sequins, and sparkly golden shoes with a pointy heel that enhanced his dance. He beamed round at the kids, and they smiled back, rather feebly wondering what was in store for them that evening.

"Have you ever heard him sing?" whispered Ruby to Mona, as they sat cross-legged in front of the stage.

"No," she admitted, "He wanted it to be a surprise for everyone."

"Shh....!" whispered Max, as the makeshift curtain began to open.

"Hey kids!" said Mr. Lion, testing and swinging the microphone around. Everyone watched, enthralled as their very own Mr. Lion spoke, his glittering get-up looking glamorous against the dark evening sky.

"I've taken to a new hobby lately, which is singing, this past month," he continued, flattered at the rapt attention on the children's faces, "And you're the first audience to listen to my singing! So, here's a fun melody of rhymes and tunes for you to jam to!"

Everyone clapped hard as he cleared his throat and the first notes of 'Mary had a little lamb' were heard. But the instant he opened his mouth to sing, everyone's hands ran up to cover their ears! He was terrible!

His voice screeched through the neighbourhood like a parrot with a sore throat and the children hated it, but did not show it at all, forcing charming smiles on their faces as they did not want to upset their beloved Mr. Lion.

The songs continued and so did the suppressed anxiety among all the kids. All this squawking and screeching brought Mr. Siberian Tiger, an old college classmate of Mr. Bear, back in Siberia, racing to their backyard. He listened in confusion for a bit and stayed, sitting behind the rows of baby animals.

Mr. Lion, not noticing anything at all, continued with full gusto as they came to 'Ten in the Bed', encouraging them to 'roll over' as in the song and join him in the chorus.

After ending 'Baa Baa Black Sheep' with a lovely decrescendo, or so thought Mr. Lion, our little friends, the Triplets started to become a little fidgety and bored. They got up, stretched their legs and excused themselves for a bit. They wandered over to the sound system behind Mr. Lion's stage.

"Woah!" exclaimed Emerald, "Look at this!"

They all ran over to her and examined the various coloured wires and hooks.

"I wonder what happens when you pull this one" pointed Ruby to a small blue wire in the corner.

And with that, she went forward and jerked it out to see what would happen. At that very moment in the show, Mr. Lion started acting extremely weird. He flung his mane around and moved abruptly rather like a robot! Everyone in the crowd thought that he was dancing superbly and with "such definition in his dance steps" as thought by Mr. Siberian Tiger. Mr. Siberian Tiger sat there, staring admiringly at Mr. Lion still doing the 'robot dance'.

It wasn't until Mrs. Lion came out with some refreshments that she saw the dance and shrieked,

" He's having an electric shock!" and ran indoors to get the kitchen broom.

She swiftly located it and rushed through the rabble of kids to the big stage, where she managed to push her husband off the stage with the broom. The Triplets, terrified, dashed back to their places and watched the whole scene in horror. At last, Mr. Lion was safely off the stage looking not much worse for his electrified spectacle up there.

The Triplets scampered up to Mrs. Lion saying, "It's all our fault! We pulled the wire behind the stage, we didn't know what would happen!" they cried into Mrs. Lion's floral apron as she patted them on their backs.

"It's alright this time little Triplets," she said, soothingly, "Just never repeat this again and never mess around with things you don't know about, okay?"

"Okay" chorused the Triplets in relief, smiling through their tears. Mr. Lion was also about to add to the conversation when suddenly Mr. Siberian Tiger marched heavily up to him.

"Hello Mr. Lion!" he roared, as he gave Mr. Lion's hand a firm shake, "I was just listening to your singing and I thought...." Everyone waited with bated breath to see if he would actually tell him the truth about his horrifying vocal ability.

"That it was wonderful!" he cried, clapping him on the back, "We Siberian Tigers are always disappointed with the drab music dished out these days , but this, he gestured, is right up our street! Especially the robot dance finale at the end was legit lit!"

"Oh really!" said Mr. Lion, most surprised to have impressed a grown-up for once. They went on talking about the evening's happenings through a delicious dinner with all the children. The Triplets smiled to themselves. They knew what they did was horribly wrong and they would never do it again, but it did get Mr. Lion a few fans. Through the suffering of poor Mr Lion, they learnt to never fiddle with unfamiliar things again, as it could lead to some disastrous dances!

Chapter 6

The Triplets Bubble Mania

It was summer. The blazing sun glared harshly upon the Ant family's tiddly ant hill, and the family was unfortunately forced to beat the heat indoors for a wearisome three months.

The Triplets, as one would expect, were absolutely devastated to learn that their home was the safest haven from the ridiculous temperatures outside, but more importantly, their mother, Mrs. Ant was rather perplexed when it dawned on her that entertaining a rowdy lot like the Triplets indoors was going to be a tall order, unlike her older and orderly children.

The first few weeks passed with relative peace, but of course, the holidays cannot stay this uneventful when you are the most riotous ripple in the pond!

"Triplets! Come here this instant!" bellowed Mr. Ant, his moon face even more disgruntled than it usually was.

The Triplets shot out of their rooms (not after creating a colossal mess in the name of a search for their water pistols) like bullets from a gun as soon as they heard their father's voice ringing through the corridor. The second they appeared under his eyes, he began once again.

"Triplets, your cousins, the ones who came over for lunch a few months ago, what were their names..." he scratched his chin in frustration.

"Oh Dad, you mean the Red Ant Triplets!" cried the Triplets, half in realisation, half in disbelief that their own father could forget his brother-in-law's children.

"Uh yes, whatever," he continued, "I've got a call from Larry, and he says that he's taking off with Larina for the day and asked me, ME out of all people to babysit those three scarlet kids of his!' he finished in one breath, his eyes as wide as saucers in utter annoyance.

"Well, Dad, you've got to handle them and us, as Mum is out shopping too and the rest of the squad are at school today!" clarified the Triplets, waiting expectantly for their dad's reaction.

"Oh bother!" he sighed, facepalming himself, whilst fanning himself with his morning Times of Antville.

The Triplets, for once, took pity on their poor, inadequate father, who was suddenly thrust upon this responsibility. They thought hard, their ribboned antennae bobbing up and down in their jewel-colours until finally, their eyes lit up in delight. They knew just the person needed for this job!

BREAKING NEWS
LOREM IPSUM
NEWSPAPER

Ding-dong, ding-dong! The sound of the shrill doorbell summoned Mr. Ant to the door, as he flung open the door hurriedly, revealing...

"Oh! Lionel!" he exclaimed, his body retracted a fraction as he glanced at the majestic figure standing patiently outside the door.

And there he was, Mr. Lion stood there placidly on the doorstep, grinning with all 30 of his massive canines, clutching an irregularly-shaped bag of goodness-knows-what.

"Come on in!" welcomed Mr Ant, more than elated that someone had come to his rescue.

Mr. Lion bestowed another Cheshire cat smile upon him and placed his furry paws on the mosaic-tiled floor.

"So, uh, Lionel..." began Mr Ant, setting out a cup of tea along with a saucer on the coffee table "You do know that my nieces will be here soon and so I better evacuate the house as quickly as possible!" he continued the last few syllables in a whisper.

"Of course!" exclaimed Mr Lion heartily, as he gulped his hot tea down in a flash, almost scorching his throat. "I've got everything I need to keep them entertained!" he explained, patting his voluminous bag by his side.

"That's quite a relief!" said Mr Ant, wiping his forehead with the back of his hand.

"Good morning Mr Lion!" chorused three little ants all crimson as each other, smiling from ear to ear.

The Triplets raced around the furniture, upsetting their mother's flower arrangement on the way, eager to meet their cousins once more. They gazed at them, heads tilted, wondering how they always happened to look neat as little pins. In matching tee-shirts and shorts, hair neatly done in pretty bows, they looked picture perfect. The Triplets were however a different story, and usually to Mrs. Ant's chagrin ended up with remnants of breakfast on their jewel-coloured outfits. Both parties smiled brightly at each other, remembering their last encounter or rather, adventure.

"This is gonna be fun!" thought the Triplets to themselves.

"Okay kids, gather round!" called Mr Lion, most authoritatively as he clapped his paws together, signalling the start of a new game.

The septet had already played numerous games, including 'Freeze Tag', 'Where's Mr Lion?', 'Pull the Red Ant Triplets Hair Ties a s Fast a s You Can' (that was the Triplet's idea, of course) and more and now they were quite exhausted and puffed in reply to Mr Lion's military call from the hall. Mr Lion, on the other hand, was having a whale of a good time with the kids, and as Mr Ant has said on many occasions, Mr Lion himself had never fully grown up, and so loved being around kids. As for Mr Ant, he deftly escaped just in time and was spending a peaceful morning outside in a cafe along with his best buddy, Mr Caterpillar.

Now in the Ant House, Mr Lion was all fired up for what he called "The Finale" of the afternoon. The six little ants encircled him, widening their eyes and stretching their feelers to see what he had brought them. Mr Lion's paws dug deep into his enormous bag and brought out.... Six magenta bubble guns!! The Triplets went quite mad with delight as they capered around the sofa, whooping for joy! The Red Ant Triplets, though, did not seem to know what the gun-like objects were.

"They're bubble guns," elucidated Mr Lion, handing them one each, "If you press the trigger bubbles will form and you can pop them if you like!"

"Wow! That sounds amazing!" they shrieked and accepted them readily. Mr Lion watched them fondly, reminiscing on his childhood days. Suddenly, he too grabbed a gun on an impulse and ran about madly, popping all the bubbles it produced. Mr Lion's bubbles were extraordinarily big compared to that of the Triplets and Red Ant Triplets. The very next moment, he blew a gargantuan bubble, so huge that it could fit all six ants quite comfortably in it. And unfortunately, it did! The Triplets and the Red Ant Triplets were wholly encompassed in the titanic bubble, their feelers wildly flapping as they scrambled around in the tight soap case.

"Hmmm, uhm, mmm!" squealed the Triplets impatiently, trying to talk through the sudsy air. Mr Lion watched in horror, as his hands ran up to cover his gaping mouth.

"Um... don't panic now, please Triplets and Red Ant Triplets!" he consoled, stutteringly, "I'll get you out of there in a jiffy!" he continued, grabbing another bubble gun, luckily at an inch, and stabbing it vigorously into the gigantic bubble.

But oh, what happened next, was totally uncalled for! Unfortunately, the bubble gun shot out another huge bubble that swallowed up Mr Lion himself! He couldn't believe his fluffy eyelids! With the six little ants in one, and Mr Lion in his very own bubble, the twin bubbles proceeded to float swiftly out the front door through the white-washed garden gate and over the lovely hedges riddled with motley flowers. They continued their journey drifting solemnly away through the streets, looking not only extremely queer but rather hilarious as well. The bubbles then bounced jauntily past the antique water fountain sitting primly on the edge of the town piazza, and finally made their way into the town plaza. As luck would have it, the ridiculous bubble-stricken septet's flight , fortunately, escaped the notice of anyone in the immediate vicinity, except for a couple of ravens who were every inch amused and also bewildered by the ginormous bubbles.

Now the bubbles eventually glided gracefully and landed smack in the middle of the town plaza, where the mayor, Mr Elephant, a distinguished, august, and respected man of the town, a politician who had never come off second-best in an election, a true veteran of the profession who had always been cut out for public service ever since he was a tiddly little trunker, was inaugurating the annual summer festival.

"And I am sincerely honoured to be inaugurating this year's Fun in The Sun Summer Festival," he rattled off, "A festival that has captured the hearts, minds, and competitive souls of... Oh My Ivories!!" he exclaimed halfway, pointing a chunky foot out at the sky, "What in the whole wide Milky Way is that!?"

The entire rabble of animals rotated their heads 180 degrees to see what their beloved mayor was ranting about. "Whatever could that be?" exclaimed the excited throng, as Mr Elephant lowered his monocle in utter disbelief.

"IT IS A UFO, you dunderhead!" shrieked Mr Elephant, busting his lungs for all he was worth, as he snapped back at his assistant Mr Crow who was readily dispatched upwards to take stock of the situation. "I was bonkers for the Spielberg guy's E.T. as a kid," he went on, getting more enthusiastic by the second, "And I would definitely know a UFO if I saw it from a million miles away!"

Well, by this time, the crowd was in a total uproar, bolting back home to retrieve cameras and phones to capture the scene. Reporters swarmed in tens, complete with camera cranes and microphones to broadcast the historic event. Mr Elephant radioed the police in two shakes of a duck's tail, to request for aid to communicate with the alien-like beings in the UFO. He sighed in satisfaction as he set the receiver down, remembering how eager he was to experience the landing of a UFO as a kid, and now how lucky he was to actually encounter one!

The police arrived, their faces beaming with delight, thrilled to be able to work on something so monumental. Just as all this commotion was building up, Mrs Ant, who was out shopping in a nearby department store, got wind of some excitement in the plaza. Excusing herself kindly from the storekeeper, she trotted outside, eyebrows raised high in interest and anticipation. As she entered the square, the first sight she saw, of course, were the hapless triplets, Red Ant Triplets and their neighbour Mr Lion, merrily floating above in what seemed to be... a bubble?!

"Triplets!!!!!!!!!!!!!" she yelled out, so loud that the walruses in Antarctica would've probably heard it in Dolby 2.0. The entire town square stared in astonishment at her, as realisation dawned slowly upon them.

"Hey", whispered Mr Giraffe to his buddy Mr Fox, "Don't they kinda look like them kids Mr Ant has?"

The whisper soon spread around the crowd, as Mr. Elephant's eyes widened in surprise and dismay at the same time.

"Ma'am, I am very sorry," he apologised profusely to Mrs Ant who was quite adamant about getting them down this instant, "We had mistaken your children and nieces and our very own Mr Lion to be alien beings in a UFO." he continued sounding exceedingly sheepish.

"Are you kidding me?!" questioned Mrs Ant, incredulously, "Those are literally my kids and my brother's kids, and our neighbour, Mr Lion!"

"Uhh yes, yes of course," stammered the mayor, pushing his feathered hat further up his head, "Our police crew will soon pop the bubbles and they will be as safe as houses, Ma'am.

The police swung into action - cranes and ladders in tow - and began to poke and prod the seemingly adamantine bubble. POP! It went and soon the residents of the bubble were safely evacuated onto the ground.

"Mum!" screamed both sets of Triplets and weirdly enough, Mr Lion as well, who was just as happy to see Mrs Ant at the scene of the crime.

The group dashed over to Mrs Ant, who was so grateful and relieved as she gave them all a huge bear hug, including poor Mr Lion who seemed to be the most shaken from the experience.

"Well, hello guys!" greeted Mr Elephant, jovially, as he strode up to them, "That's been quite an adventure hasn't it?" he questioned, grinning cheekily.

"It sure has been Mister Mayor!" chorused the Triplets, looking none the worse for their bubble stunt.

"Just wanted to tell you all something," the mayor said, leaning in closer, "these bubbles could earn us quite a pretty penny if we were to open it as an adventure sports activity in these parts, you know."

"It is indeed an innovative business idea Mr Mayor." interjected the scholarly Red Ant Triplets.

"Well then, we have to celebrate the inventor!" he exclaimed, "Who invented this marvel?"

"It was Mr Lion, Mr Lion!" called out the Triplets, shoving an extremely red-faced and embarrassed Mr Lion to the front of the group.

"Actually, uh, yes, this disaster was my creation ," confessed Mr Lion truthfully. Mr Elephant walked over to him and shook his paw so firmly, that it would have fallen off Lionel's arm.

"Thank you, Lionel! You may be the next entertainment tycoon with an invention like that, you never know!" congratulated the Mayor.

And the two of them hurried away to Mr Elephant's office to discuss the ins and outs of it all. The Triplets, clutching their mother's hand rather tightly , watched with an amused smile on their faces. At the end of the day, a lot of conclusions could be made of course but they think the salient one of them all, would be to never let Mr Lion babysit them ever again!

Chapter 7

The Triplets at the Theatre

It was a chilly evening one November weekend and the Falls family was slated to go into the big theatre in the Jungle centre to enjoy a famous play by the great dramatist Shakespeare or as the Triplets called him with their adorable lisp, 'Saekspeer' of whom Pink and Orange were big fans.

"The seat numbers are 33, 34, 35, 36, 37, 38, 39, 40, 41," said Mr. Ant, peering at the tickets in the dim light of the grand auditorium.

"Pass them to me dear," said Mrs. Ant briskly, perusing the tickets meticulously, "We nearly took Mr and Mrs Giraffe's seats!" she scolded, lightly tapping her bewildered husband's arm as she nudged him to the row of seats on their right.

The triplets gave a gleeful giggle! They were finally here! After their afternoon nap time, they dressed in warm jumpers and woolly hats, and hopped in the car and now the show was about to begin!

"Mummy," they asked, "Can we take the edge seats, please?"

"Alright," replied their mother, thinking nothing of the request, as she glanced around to ensure that all nine of them were seated comfortably. Assured that everything was at peace, she took her seat and sighed in relaxation. The triplets grinned contentedly. Now whenever they wanted to, they could walk around without disturbing anyone, as they could not bear to sit like a statue for the next two hours.

"Shh triplets, you have to be quiet !" hushed their older sister Niagara Falls.

The curtains opened and the pageant began with sprightly song and dance with the characters all in bright mediaeval costumes. It was actually entertaining at first but as the show progressed the Triplets' amusement petered out and they were soon restive and bored. They concluded that it would really do no harm to just have a quick look about.

"Sapphire, Emerald!" whispered Ruby, "Plan B- is in action!"

"Right on!" hyped the other two and as smooth as a puma on the prowl, they crept out of their chairs.

Once they had exited the main auditorium, they climbed a flight of steps and turned into an empty corridor. They trotted along the corridor and came across a dazzling hall full of mirrors.

They leaned back a good ninety degrees, eyes widened in curiosity at the surreal surroundings. They flocked inside to look. Apart from shimmering walls, there was an array of costumes and props of every kind. It looked like a museum they had seen in a movie.

Soon enough, they were all over the place exploring all that they could find.

They clambered up the counters and their tiddly selves looked amazed at the seemingly boundless assortment of brightly coloured tins and tubs in all shapes and sizes.

"Ooh!" exclaimed Sapphire, "This one's full of the same powder Mummy puts on us."

She put the lid back on hurriedly as she soon had a coughing fit.

"Ooh, how do I look?" gushed Ruby, already trying on a pink tiara and scepter.

Just as they were beginning to really enjoy their new adventure, Emerald spotted a silhouetted figure in the hallway. A shiver of fear crept up her spine, as she tiptoed to gain a better vantage point. She peered at the hallway getting as close as she dared. But as the figure sailed away, she soon dismissed the matter from her mind, thinking It was merely her eyes playing tricks. She returned hastily and joined the others in their new silly game. But soon, the massive figure appeared again and this time it walked straight into the room! The Triplets froze in terror. It towered over the little trio with its silver armour and helmet glinting eerily under the lights.

"Run for it!" yelled Ruby as they sprinted through the corridor and down the stairs tripping over some of them in their hurry. But strangely enough, the figure walked calmly down the stairs and followed them! After running for what seemed like years, all down the staircase and through the halls, the Triplets halted sharply and looked around them. The figure was nowhere in sight!

"I think we lost him!" panted Sapphire, wiping her sweaty forehead with the back of her palm. But as soon as she uttered those words, they heard the clanking of the metal again and were about to gallop for their lives, when they heard a peculiar whistling sound floating straight from the figure.

"Are you alright?" asked Ruby, forgetting her apparent fright for a minute, thinking him stranger than ever. Then suddenly, he lifted a piece of his armour and the Triplets watched with bated breath until they noticed a face inside... a large but pleasant gorilla face.

He guffawed and finally spoke, "It's okay kids, I'm no monster! I'm just dressed in armour as a soldier for the play."

The Triplets stayed rooted to the ground and finally, realisation dawned on them. And all of a sudden, they too saw the funny side and they all began to giggle while reprimanding themselves in jest for being such scaredy-cats!

"Well," said the friendly gorilla, trying to catch his breath after the intense and long laughter session, "You'd better run along before you miss the rest of the show!"

"Oh yes!" exclaimed the Triplets, "We forgot all about it!"

They bolted straight to the auditorium and slipped into their seats once again. Fortunately for them, the rest of the family had been so engrossed in the play that they hadn't even noticed they were gone! The triplets heaved a great sigh of relief and calmly enjoyed the remainder of the show.

After the show was over, people lined up in hundreds outside the theatre in big queues to take pictures with and collect autographs from the actors.

"Triplets!" called Angel Falls, "Do you want to take a picture with the soldier? Apparently, he's a super famous actor."

"We'd rather not, thank you!" winced the Triplets as they scuttled past him in embarrassment. Then, they drove away to their favourite cafe for a lovely dinner and finally home to hit the sack.

Their theatre adventure was obviously not the best way to kill boredom, but they will surely think twice before even envisioning any more walkabouts!

Chapter 8

The Triplets Go Shopping

As the months flew by, the Triplets had begun to collect a potpourri of experiences, each one more hair-raising than the previous one. They had already been to numerous restaurants, a railway station, and even the theatre, leaving Mrs Ant feeling like she was on her last legs! Just when she firmly decided that the Triplets would stay put at home and enjoy the tranquillity of lovely October autumn with the rest of the family, the Triplets were unexpectedly gifted with another outing, this time, to the Jungle's most luxurious shopping complex.

"Dear," called Mr Ant one cloudy afternoon, as he sprawled lazily on his sofa, flicking aimlessly through his leftover morning newspaper, "We've been invited to Lionel's birthday party the day after tomorrow ," he informed, as he turned around to face his wife.

"The day after tomorrow?!" yelped Mrs Ant in alarm, eyebrows raised higher than the Twins' number of encyclopedias. "That means we need to buy him a present soon then!" she realised a fraction of a second later, running her hands through her feelers in distress.

"I suppose..." mumbled Mr Ant, still reading his newspaper, his spectacles dangling precariously off the tip of his nose. Privately, he presumed that it was much too silly of an adult to expect a present on his birthday, even though Mr Ant himself was as delighted as a three-year-old every year on his birthday.

At this point in the conversation, the Triplets had just sauntered into the living room for a snack, hands dug deep into the pockets of their tiny overalls as they just finished a spot of finger-painting on the back porch.

"How about," began Ruby thoughtfully, as she rubbed her chin, "We get him that microphone set that he's been dreaming about recently?" she suggested.

"Of course!" exclaimed Sapphire, slapping her sister's back in agreement.

"He does love singing, no cap!" interjected Emerald, as her father looked positively shaken by the mere thought of even spending an extra cent on a 35-year-old's birthday present.

"Well that's settled then!" smiled Mrs Ant in relief. "Since you three know exactly what he wants, we'll head off to Jungle Central first thing tomorrow!"

"Alright, now Triplets, stay close to me and don't wander anywhere! Is that understood?" commanded Mrs Ant, as she pulled the three little ants closer to herself in the elevator of Jungle Central. They had just entered the local mall, but all the Triplets could notice were the whiffs of cinnamon pastries wafting deliciously from the nearby Mole in One bakery. Animals of all shapes and sizes scuttled around hurriedly, while others strolled casually through the enormous avenues that parted the shops into two rows.

Mrs Ant immediately whirled them into a brightly-lit store that seemingly encompassed the whole world's wardrobes into one place.

"Mummy, why are we here?" questioned Emerald, looking up at her mother with a puzzled expression.

"Well," replied Mrs Ant, "Since we're here, I figured that we'd better buy you all a couple of T-shirts and shoes as you absolutely destroyed the ones you wore while painting yesterday and the rest of your outfits look pretty much the same," she explained patiently, as she carefully examined the rows of squeaky sneaker shoes and then quickly decided against it, remembering how the Triplets squeaked the life out of them plus the patience of the entire neighbourhood three months ago.

While Mrs Ant leisurely browsed the wide and varied kids' clothing collection, the Triplets, as always, were curious to explore. So, while their mother was in deep conversation about the sale offer for 'children under one' with a helpful, stout otter, the Triplets easily stole to the other side of the shop, their jewel-coloured shoes making no noise as they scampered away.

They wandered rather slowly through the whole place, taking it all in, as they looked through racks and rows of dresses, pants, t-shirts, shorts and jumpsuits, all hanging on their respective hangers and glaring down at the tiny frames of the Triplets. The Triplets, however, remained unabashed and began to play a riotous game of Hide and Seek between the curtains of clothes.

"How long is she counting for?" whispered Sapphire furiously, as she momentarily peeped around the corner of her hiding spot. It was now their fourth round of the game and Ruby, who was perennially proclaimed 'it', was supposed to commence her search for the others. Finally, her persistence was rewarded, when she heard the unmistakable whoop of joy from the other aisle, as Ruby immediately found Emerald and dragged her mercilessly out of her hideout, while they both laughed hysterically. Sapphire, completely forgetting that she was still hidden, shrieked with delight and unwittingly let herself out of the bag! Shoppers passed by, up and down the aisles, not noticing anything wrong, as many children do tend to play in stores whilst their parents shop. They were having so much fun that they didn't realise when a particular shopper was in their vicinity.

As they were giggling uncontrollably together like a pack of hyenas, Ruby suddenly stopped and pointed at a rather familiar figure in the distance, as her eyebrows furrowed in confusion.

"Isn't that...Mr Lion?!" she gasped in realisation, her hand flying up to cover her open mouth. The others rotated their heads so quickly that Emerald nearly twisted hers off, as they strained their necks to see what Ruby was so shaken about.

"It is!" confirmed Sapphire in a too-loud voice.

"We can't let him know we're here!" said Emerald, "Otherwise he'll ask us what we're here for and we'll have to spill the tea about his present!" she continued, shoving the others into a rack of Bermuda shorts.

"Quick, hide! He's coming closer!" urged Ruby, as they darted around the store, in fervent pursuit of a fool-proof hiding place. Suddenly, Emerald had a brainwave. She rapidly called the others over to the tiddly mannequins, standing stolidly in the shop window and with all her might, pushed them over so that they could not be seen anymore.

"Stand still and don't breathe," she ordered them seriously.

Well, as you can probably tell, the ingenious trio stood in place of the three ant mannequins in the shop window! Amazingly, their faces were as stony as the Statue of Liberty's herself and they propped themselves up stylishly, posing better than any runway model, each with a pair of borrowed sunglasses from the former mannequins, who now lay lifeless on the floor.

Sure enough, Mr Lion ambled closer, languidly pushing his half-empty trolley along the aisles, trying to remember exactly what shade of pink bows Mona had instructed him to buy for the party earlier that morning. The Triplets stiffened in their positions, hardly daring to even breathe, as they widened their eyes to avoid even the slightest blink. Unfortunately, luck was not on their side that day, as Mr Lion did not just casually pass them by as they hoped, but instead, was determined to stay rooted to his spot in front of the shop's window display and stared mystified into it.

The Triplets stared right back, hearts pumping loudly inside their tiny chests, as Mr Lion beckoned to the aforementioned otter staff who readily hurried over to assist him. The Triplets grimaced internally while trying to not move even their toenails. This was turning out to be harder than they ever imagined. From what they could decipher, (Sapphire was allegedly a self-taught lip-reader) Mr Lion was interested in buying the clothes on the mannequins in lion cub size for Mona, but the poor otter, as much as he studied the three mannequins in front of him, could not seem to place those clothes anywhere in the huge store.

Mr. Lion had apparently lost patience and proceeded to head toward the check-out counters when a sudden intrusive thought hit him,

"Have I seen those mannequins before?" he thought to himself, feeling like he had seen those exact same mannequins along with the clothes before. However, he quickly shook himself, convinced that the deja vu was merely a result of his previous late-night as he had spent a merry night recording songs in Mr Pink Panther's studio.

The Triplets, on the other hand, were so very relieved the second they saw Mr Lion drive his trolley over to the exit and were just about to step down from the mannequins' platform when someone else decided to pass by... Mrs Ant! They shivered in fear, as their very own mother wheeled her trolley closer and closer to the window display. She immediately caught sight of the peculiar-looking mannequins who seemed impressively life-like. She frowned slightly as she stepped forward, slowly recognising the clothes on the three statues.

"Triplets?!" she whisper-shouted, as the corners of their mouths immediately turned upwards into a sheepish trio of smiles. Mrs Ant could hardly believe what she was seeing. Her own Triplets were at it again, pretending to be mannequins in a shop window . Whatever could happen next?

"Get down from there!" she said, teeth gritted in frustration, as they instantly climbed down faster than lightning, to be met with an increasingly exasperated mother.

Needless to say, the Triplets were promptly escorted outside the shop, not without slipping into the electronics store to buy Mr Lion's birthday present, of course. Just as they were exiting the mall, she stopped by the staff of the clothes store to apologise for any damage her faux mannequins had done to the real ones.

"Oh, no problem at all, Mrs Ant, no problem at all!" assured Mr Kangaroo, the manager of the store, as she shook her hand vigorously with a beaming smile, which caused not only her but the Triplets to also be utterly confused.

"In fact," he continued, bouncing up and down in excitement, as most kangaroos do involuntarily when they get hyped. "Your triplets in the shop window have increased sales by more than half in just one day!" he exclaimed, still bouncing merrily, as the Triplets tried hard to control their peals of laughter.

"Everyone was absolutely astounded by the smart window display and loved it! Your three might even have a career as child models!" said Mr Kangaroo, finally firmly on the ground.

"Why thank you, Mr Kangaroo" replied Mrs Ant politely, as she glanced round at her three 'future models' squirming uncomfortably behind her floral dress.

The following day at the party, Mr. Lion was completely bowled over and touched by the Ant family's present to him, even if Mr Ant was a tad bit salty about his pocket becoming considerably lighter. He also happened to recount a recent experience that he was reminded of as he saw the Triplets,

"Triplets, do you know there are mannequins that look like Xerox copies of you in Jungle Junction's main department store?" he commented, as he popped the collar of his new tuxedo, obviously very much in love with himself that evening.

" Oh, that sounds cool!" replied the Triplets, as mischievous smiles formed on their faces, "We'd love to see them too!"

Chapter 9

Mr. Lion Goes to the Cinema

The Triplets were now well into their toddler years and started to develop new hobbies and interests...besides food. You see, a year ago, the Ant family along with their close friends and neighbours, the Lion family flocked to the cinemas to watch an all-new animated film, Meowana. Well, ever since then, the triplets love trooping to the cinema in their tiddly, little SUV and the whole atmosphere of the movies in general - bright, flashing lights glimmering all around, the scent of freshly popped popcorn wafting through the air and the scintillating movies that serenade the audience. For a wonder - aside from their initial encounter with theatres, they managed to stay right out of trouble and quite behaved themselves - much to Mrs. Ant's delight. But now, the pandemic of COVID-19 not only struck humans like you and me, but most unfortunately, the Jungle world as well! The doors were shut firmly to all shopping malls, cinemas and restaurants and boy, did this not go well with the triplets! They just blew up in smoke as they couldn't visit any places, arrange play-dates with their best friends and couldn't even stroll down to the ice cream shop for jewel-coloured popsicles! Life seemed rather unfair to the poor unwary threesome! But, as always, life doesn't stay monotonous for long when you are the most disruptive trio in the Jungle...

"Mummy! Mummy!" hollered the Triplets through the halls cupping their hands over their mouths and dangling a piece of paper in the air.

Mrs. Ant, who was peacefully enjoying her third cup of coffee (a side effect of mothering the Trips) and reading a book titled 'How to Parent Spirited Kids' was rudely interrupted and jumped to her feet, fearing what her troublesome triad was up to now.

"Whatever is the matter?" she cried, flapping her palms down, trying to calm the overenthusiastic triplets.

"The cinemas are opening and so are the restaurants and others!" they gushed in excitement.

"Ah I see," she replied, taking the newspaper from them.

"Wow Triplets, this is the first time you've ever shown interest in reading!" remarked their father, Mr. Ant, most sarcastically as he skimmed through the movie reviews along with Mrs. Ant.

"Very funny, Daddy" growled the Triplets folding their arms.

"Oh, Tripsy dears," said Mrs. Ant, "You can only enter if you are vaccinated..."

"What?!" asked the Triplets inquisitively.

"Vaccinated," repeated Mr. Ant, "It means you are safer from the virus but you cannot take the vaccine unless you are above 12 years old." he continued, blankly.

Well, this practically pricked the entire balloon of their enthusiasm! They burst into a fountain of tears and bellowed through the house! Mr. and Mrs. Ant turned to each other unhappily. Trying to soothe the wounds, Mr. Ant inquired,

"Um... was there a particular movie you wanted to see, Trips?".

"Yes!" they wailed in despair, "It was 'The Carnival of Animals' with an awesome display of baby animals!".

"Oh....", said Mr. Ant, who obviously had absolutely no idea of the entertainment avenues of kids nowadays. "Perhaps we can stream it on Nestflix or Amazon Climb?" he offered.

"No Daddy, it's not available anywhere!" they cried and snorted noisily into a pile of tissues.

Mrs. Ant, who had been watching these proceedings for a while, thought of something marvellous at just that moment.

"What if," she pondered out loud, "We send an adult who is vaccinated to watch the movie for you, triplets? That way, he or she can relate to you everything that happened in the film."

"That's a great idea!" exclaimed the Triplets, jumping up from the sofa and upsetting the mountain of tissues over Mr. Ant.

"Yes," said Mr. Ant, slowly as he pulled the tissues off himself, "And I happen to know just the right creature for the job."

"WHAT?!!!!!" roared Mr. Lion into the receiver, that evening, making Mrs. Lion drop her freshly baked cookies.

She stayed rooted to her spot watching her husband's furry face progressively get redder and hotter.

"Whatever is the matter, dear?" she asked as soon as he hung up the phone. Mr. Lion took a deep breath and blurted out, "Mr. Ant wants me to watch a movie at the multiplex for the Triplets but it's Covid out there and you know how scared I am of that, right!"

This was all said in one breath and sounded like a bunch of gobbledygook to Mrs. Lion. Eventually, she got the message loud and clear: Mr. Lion agreed to go to the cinema, because he could not disappoint the Triplets and now was terrified to go.

"It's okay, dear, you know how even Mona and Max are dying to see that film and this year's been a rough one for all the baby animals in the jungle," she consoled, as she patted him on the back.

"Well, I guess they would appreciate it, wouldn't they?" reasoned Mr. Lion, cocking his large head to one side.

"I'm sure they will, positive!" said Mrs. Lion, smiling.

"Oh well, then I'm going!" declared Mr. Lion with a determined look on his face and teeth gritted, and then realised that Mrs. Lion had just exited the room and he was alone. Feeling rather stupid, he hurriedly sat down.

"Name please, and movie", demanded the cashier at the cinema.

The cinema looked none worse for its long vacation away from the public. The huge red billboards were illuminated with dozens of lights and the smell of soft drinks and popcorn floated through the dim halls as vaccinated animals filled the theatres. Mr. Lion, clothed in complete PPE (Personal Protective Equipment), duly gave his name and movie and received his personal ticket.

He stood outside Screen 13 and peered inside. He took a step forward and then two rapidly back. This repeated for quite a long while until finally he decided to enter. He fumbled in the darkness for his seat as numerous animals stared at his peculiar attire, which rather looked as if he had to come to view a Star Trek movie! He sprayed disinfectant on his seat and wiped it thoroughly. He gazed at it once more with utmost scrutiny as though he were counting the germs lurking in there! He finally decided to ascend the throne and sat comfortably. A striped, lanky zebra advanced towards him and took a seat a couple of places away. Mr. Lion grimaced slightly but then shifted his glance to the large screen, where the movie was about to begin.

The movie was undoubtedly a gem of a film! It had Mr. Lion on the edge of his seat for almost the entire time, except when he dropped his 3D glasses on the carpeted floor and had to grope about looking for them. At last, the movie was done and the flashing lights gleamed once again. He sighed in satisfaction and proceeded to wend his way through the seats and out the door. Just as he was strolling outside, wondering if it was time for a post-movie snack, a piercing alarm bell rang through the building and stopped Mr. Lion in his tracks. A burly bull attendant came up to him and inquired urgently,

"Did you just come out of Theatre 13?"

"Yes...yes, I just watched a film there" stuttered Mr. Lion, oblivious to what was happening.

"Well, then you'll have to come with me, sir" bellowed the attendant and Mr. Lion followed, meek as a lamb.

"Wh-what's this all about?" asked Mr. Lion, in despair. The bull clicked his tongue impatiently and answered,

"A mongoose reported a case of coronavirus from a zebra sitting to her left who apparently was coughing all the time!".

"Zebra!" screamed Mr. Lion, " He was on my right!".

"Exactly" continued the bull, "He's been sent for testing and you guys need to be tested and isolated as well." Goodness, gracious! Wasn't this just what Mr. Lion being afraid of? He moaned loudly and gave a wail of disappointment. Mr. Bull eventually turned into a lane of testing cubicles and left a shivering Mr. Lion in one of them. A nurse popped her head around and saw Mr. Lion in one of them trembling and sniffing despondently. She was just about to prepare a swab for him when her supervisor called for her. She ran across to him and came back grinning from ear to ear.

"Sir," she began to Mr. Lion.

"Oh hello, yes I am ready" he responded with a lugubrious face as if he were going to battle.

"Actually Sir," the nurse went on, "I am happy to inform you that the suspected case was confirmed as negative, it seems the zebra was coughing only because kernels from the popcorn got stuck in his throat!" she concluded, with a smile. Mr. Lion stared at her in disbelief.

Then he gave a whoop of joy and leapt up from his chair in glee! Hollering a profuse 'Thank you' to the nurse and supervisor, he skipped his way out of the mall and flung himself into his giant SUV, earning quite a few glances of disapproval but nothing could abate his spirit at this moment.

He sped back home and carefully bathed himself from top to toe and spent an hour and a half, sanitising his face and hands. After his elaborate disinfection, he sauntered over to the Ant family's house, eager to enlighten them on the movie.

" Hallo Mr. Lion!" exclaimed Mr. Ant as he opened the door and shook his hand jovially.

"Hey, Mr. Lion!" chanted the triplets, walking into the living room. Mrs. Lion, Mona and Max were also at the Ant household, having a playdate and longing to hear all about the movie. Mr. Lion seated himself on a soft, fabric sofa and the five babies sat in a circle at his feet.

"Ahh..." said Mr. Lion, stretching his hands and feet and tail.

"Tell us about the movie Mr. Lion!" urged the children impatiently.

"Wait a bit, kids, let Mr. Lion first tell us about how his trip went ," said Mr. Ant, nodding towards his friend.

"Er... yes, of course." stammered Mr. Lion, not sure of what to say. As he began to relate the jarring events surrounding his day at the movies both parents and children listened with bated breath, not daring to halt the shocking episode until it concluded. At the end of it all, Mr. Lion looked round at his admiring audience and laughed.

"Now would you like to hear about the movie, kids?" he asked rhetorically.

"As a matter of fact, Mr. Lion," said the Triplets grinning most cheekily, " The movie would never be half as interesting as the story you've just told us!". Everyone erupted into laughter as Mr. Lion smiled contentedly. And I hope you did too!

Chapter 10

The Triplets First Birthday

The Triplets' days were now quite smooth sailing and on an even keel and they had remained relatively good for quite a long period of time. Well, no one thought that much surprising as they really were getting older now. Though hard to believe, it was nearly a year since that December morning they were born. And this is where we find the Triplets today....

"Good morning Triplets!" wished Mrs. Ant pleasantly as she drew open the jewel-coloured curtains of the bedroom.

"Morning, Mum!" cried the Triplets as they sat up, one by one, rubbing their eyes and tumbling out of bed in their polka-dotted pajamas. "Do you know what day it is today?" asked their mum, as she sat comfortably beside them.

They frowned and shook their antennae left and right.

"Well, it's the day before your birthday!" she answered happily.

'Our birthday is tomorrow?!" they questioned incredulously, as the trio had actually no idea when they were born.

"Yes!" replied Mrs. Ant, while they clapped their hands in glee, their mischievous eyes gleaming with sheer excitement. "And today I shall zip down to the store to buy decorations for your party tomorrow evening!" she continued.

The Triplets shrieked in delight! They had attended a caboodle of birthday parties among the jungle children and now it was finally their turn! They combed their feelers, brushed their teeth and were soon at breakfast gobbling down their meal like a pack of hyenas. The entire family joined them a moment later and while they ate, they discussed plans for their youngest ones' birthday.

" So, Triplets, what flavour of cake would you fancy?" questioned Angel Falls, as she reached out for a pen and a piece of paper to write it down.

"Oh, um..." thought the Triplets as if it was the most important decision of their itty-bitty lives. "Maybe chocolate, butterscotch and vanilla! One flavour for each one of us!" they answered quite reasonably.

"Oh yeah, that makes sense ," said Angel Falls as she seemed a bit startled at the gigantic order. As the meal concluded, Mrs. Ant readied herself for her shopping trip and headed out the door to the department store, Paws and Tails.

After their mother left, the Triplets were left all alone as their four other sisters were rather busy themselves. They dawdled aimlessly through the great house, bumping into quite a few sisters on the way. Lastly, they bumped into sister numero dos, Niagara Falls, who was genuinely shocked at her sisters' boredom.

"Hey Triplets, I forgot to ask you, but are you making any return gifts for your party guests?" she asked, her eyebrows furrowed in curiosity.

"Return gifts?" inquired the Triplets, a quizzical look plastering their faces.

"Yeah, it's a way to thank your guests after they attend your party." she responded, "So you have to make them each something small today."

"Oh...thanks!" exclaimed the Triplets, delighted to find themselves set on a brand-new project, or knowing the Triplets, an adventure.

"Now, what do you think we should make?" pondered Ruby, taking charge of the trio immediately, as they sat like a row on their peach three-seater sofa.

"Cards?" suggested Sapphire, as they nodded in approval a millisecond later.

"Not a bad idea, actually, Sapphire." complimented Ruby. Sapphire automatically showed all her teeny ivories and sat back in satisfaction. Emerald suddenly upset the philosophical atmosphere by standing up and announcing that she was heading to the kitchen to get something to munch on so that she could think better. They all promptly followed her like chicks behind a mother hen, into the cool lemon-yellow kitchen. Just as they were about to take a humongous bite out of the muffins they managed to salvage out of the bottom shelf of the fridge, Ruby abruptly banged the table hard, making the other two Trips jump.

"What's up Ruby?" asked her sisters, quite astonished by her intensity. "Why don't we make cupcakes as return gifts?" proposed Ruby, excitedly, reading the room carefully for the others' reactions.

"Perfect!" they cried out, hi-fiving each other.

"But who's going to bake them for us?" realised Emerald, with a blank expression on her face.

"Oh Emerald, we've watched Mummy do this at least a hundred times already!" convinced Sapphire, "I'm sure we can pull it off ourselves by now!"

"That's the spirit!" said Ruby enthusiastically as they all leapt up for a tri-five!

"Okay, now I want everyone to concentrate," commanded Ruby, dictatorially, "What do we need first?"

"Oh, oh," stuttered Sapphire, "What's it called again, um, flour!"

"Flowers?" questioned Emerald, scratching her head hard.

"Oh yes, of course, flowers." confirmed Ruby, "I'll just slip outside to pick some!"

And with that, she marched out of the kitchen and ran into the garden and picked some beautiful bunches of gladiolus, roses and buttercups. She gathered them in her arms and dashed back into the kitchen.

"Done!" she cried, plucking the stems off and throwing them higgledy-piggledy all around the kitchen.

"Those look great!" approved Emerald, glancing briefly at them. Now, all the flowers were neatly arranged in a bowl.

"I think we need to whisk it now," thought Sapphire out loud, as they added half-cracked soggy eggs to the mixture.

"Right on it!" said Emerald and fetched the electric whisk.

"Good, now all we have to do is press the button and woah!" That was Ruby, obviously, the 'woah' was because the whisk was now out of control and the gooey mixture was flying all over the countertops and themselves. Finally, Ruby remembered to press the stop button and all calm was restored in a moment.

"Phew!" she sighed, flicking bits of eggshell off herself.

"Oh, nice! It's all whisked now!" chimed Sapphire, peering mysteriously into the bowl. The batter, if you could call it so, stared back, orangey-yellow in colour.

"Does it usually look like this?" asked Emerald, in disbelief, as their three tiny heads studied the batter. Ruby gave it a slight stir to check.

"It's all fine! " she declared, and the rest of them gave little sighs of relief. They all immediately proceeded to poke one finger in it and lick the batter off them.

"Ooh!" they smiled at each other, as it was very nice, but rather too sweet, but obviously they did not mind.

"Actually, do you think we need to add some chocolate?" asked Ruby, seeking the others' approval.

"Yeah sure, a little chocolate never hurt anyone!" commented Sapphire, bouncing up to ferret out the cocoa tin.

"Chuck it here," called Emerald, "I'll pour it in."

"Sure, catch!" said Sapphire. Emerald put her hands out, poised for the catch, but, oh dear, somehow or the other it slipped out of her hands and landed on the tiled floor, spilling heaps of brown dust that coated the Triplets from feeler to toe! They coughed and sputtered all over each other and picked up the offending tin, which was almost empty now.

" Umm... you know what, let's just collect the cocoa off the floor and dump it in the bowl!" suggested Sapphire. They then threw all the powder into their large mixing bowl. They gave it another disastrous whisk and finally got out the muffin tray.

"This is going really well!" assured Ruby, as they filled the muffin moulds with the now nearly mud-coloured batter, mottled with hues of orange, yellow and pink.

"Now all we have to do is shove them in the oven and then they're good to go!" exclaimed Emerald, opening the over door. Resting the tray with their mother's best baking mitts , they gently placed it in the oven and shut it close. After the success of their 'beautiful' cupcakes, they quietly retired to the living room to skim through their new comics with a sweet sense of accomplishment. So peacefully, in fact, that they completely forgot about their precious return gifts, sweltering in the oven!

After about an hour or so, Mrs. Ant came home, pleasantly tired from all her shopping and was about to announce to the Triplets that she was home when the smell of something burning greeted her at the door.

She followed the acrid smell and it led her directly to the kitchen, and oh my, when she flung open the door, what a shock she got! Flowers stems strewn everywhere, egg-shells adorning the countertops, the floor plastered in coloured batter and of course, the oven nearly bursting ajar!

A swarm of thoughts rushed through her head, but the only one that showed up in neon lights was... the Triplets! She hurried to the oven and opened it with arms flailing to fight off the smoke it emitted. As she pulled the muffin tray closer, she recognized what it was.

"Triplets!!!!!" she screamed, as the door banged shut.

The Triplets came running hastily and asked frantically, "What happened Mum?" At the sight of their mum's thunderous face and the state of the kitchen, they grimaced and squirmed uncomfortably.

Naturally, they were made to tell their mother the entire story from beginning to end and though she tried determinedly to keep a straight face the whole time, she had to let out a giggle or two. Amends were soon in progress: Angel and Niagara took over the making of the return gifts, while Mrs. Ant and the Triplets cleaned up the kitchen in the meantime.

The next day was their birthday and they had a whale of a good time and were gifted all sorts of wonderful presents. At the party, Mona and Max Lion did ask what had happened to all the flowers in their garden. They simply smiled, winked at each other and reassured them that the flowers had been used for an extremely noble cause.

The Triplets have had an extremely chaotic, ridiculous and hilarious first year of their lives, as seen through the book. They are glad that you could join them on their hair-raising adventures too! Even though this is the end of the book, this is not the end of the Triplets; as long as you can play with them in your imagination!

Vocab Challenge
Did you know?

Chapter 1: Welcome to the World, Triplets!

1. chilly- very cold
2. aroma- good smell
3. wafting- pass gently through the air (usually a good smell or sounds)
4. presuming- to suppose
5. bamboozled- to be surprised because the person has been cheated or fooled
6. hallmark- a distinctive feature
7. trepidation- a feeling of fear or anxiety
8. unceremonious- lack of proper manner or dignity
9. viability- ability to live or survive successfully
10. assess- to check or evaluate
11. pint-sized- tiny
12. slated- expected to be

Chapter 2: The Triplets Show Themselves Around

1. doting- to be extremely fond of
2. rambunctious- very boisterous

3. absurdity- ridiculous or wildly unreasonable
4. placid- not easily upset
5. tall order- a difficult task
6. monotonous- boring or repetitive
7. precariously- in a way that is not secure or likely to fall/collapse
8. adorn- to make more beautiful
9. haven- a place of safety or refuge
10. bewilderment- a feeling of being very confused
11. prodigious- greatly abnormal

<u>Chapter 3: Meeting the Red Ant Triplets</u>

1. best bet- safest or most reliable course of action
2. Impish- inclined to do naughty things for fun
3. wrap wool around someone's eyes- to trick
4. sparky- lively and high-spirited
5. quizzical- feeling of being mildly puzzled
6. proffer- to hold out in front of someone
7. secluded- not seen by many people; private
8. alcove- small, private space in a room
9. apple-pie order- perfect organisation and neatness
10. prominent- important
11. radar- a person's ability to sense events, factors etc.

12. crane- stretch out one's neck or body
13. cascade- to pour downwards in large quantities
14. stifle- to restrain an action
15. pristine- clean and fresh
16. gaily- in a cheerful or light-hearted way
17. gingerly- in a careful or cautious manner
18. trivial- of little value or importance
19. pursuit- the act of following or chasing something
20. havoc- chaos
21. foreign- strange and unfamiliar
22. shrill- high pitched and piercing
23. in a tizzy- state of agitation
24. helter-skelter- in disorder or confusion
25. cower- crouch down in fear

Chapter 4: The Triplets First Getaway

1. pique- to feel irritated
2. topsy-turvy- upside down
3. disgruntled- dissatisfied
4. propose- to suggest
5. jolt- shake abruptly
6. distressed- to be extremely anxious
7. noir- black
8. unintended- not planned or meant

9. duly- following proper routine
10. jovial- good-humoured or cheerful
11. escapade- adventure
12. squiggly- wavy or twisty
13. motley- a variety of colours
14. sumptuous- many or plenty
15. reverie- state of being pleasantly lost in one's thoughts
16. jarring- striking
17. unbeknownst- without the knowledge of someone
18. pickle- a difficult situation

Chapter 5: Mr Lion's Listening Party

1. hiccup- minor problem
2. reputed- widely known and well thought of
3. vigorously- full of energy
4. theatrical- excessively dramatic
5. slick- make one's hair flat
6. reinforce- to strengthen
7. smother- restrain an expression or emotion
8. eccentric- unconventional and slightly strange
9. gone bonkers- to lose one's sanity
10. catnip- substance given to cats which makes them overly excited
11. roly-poly- having a round, plump appearance

12. rummage- to search untidily
13. to wend one's way- to walk to a certain place
14. turquoise- greenish-blue colour
15. arguing with a brick wall- an argument in which the person whom you are talking to does not listen
16. jaws dropped ten feet- state of complete shock
17. feebly- in a way that lacks strength or force
18. makeshift- a temporary or primitively made arrangement
19. enthral- to capture the fascinated attention of
20. rapt- completely fascinated or absorbed
21. screech- loud, harsh, piercing cry
22. suppress- to restrain
23. fidgety- restless or uneasy
24. rabble- a disorderly crowd
25. bated breath- nervous or anxious state

Chapter 6: The Triplets' Bubble Mania

1. tiddly- tiny
2. wearisome- bored or tired
3. rowdy- noisy and disorderly
4. riotous- wild and uncontrolled
5. colossal- huge
6. inadequate- lacking the qualifications for a certain task

7. retract- draw back
8. scorch- burn something with fire or heat
9. chagrin- annoyance or distress
10. voluminous- very loose or full
11. magenta- dark pink-red colour
12. reminisce- remember happy memories
13. at inch- closeby
14. riddled- to be filled with
15. piazza- a public square or marketplace
16. every inch- thoroughly or completely
17. august- respected and impressive
18. veteran- person who has lots of experience in a certain field
19. inaugurate- to begin or introduce
20. rattle- to talk in a lively, rapid way
21. chunky- bulky and thick
22. throng- crowd
23. monocle- a single eyeglass
24. dunderhead- a stupid person
25. dispatch- send off to a destination for a purpose
26. hapless- unfortunate
27. adamantine- unable to be broken
28. adamant- refuse to be persuaded or to change one's mind
29. sheepish- embarrassed or shameful

30. incredulously- in a manner of disbelief
31. pretty penny- lots of money
32. tycoon- a wealthy, powerful person in business or industry
33. scholarly- having or showing knowledge of academic pursuits
34. salient- most noticeable or important

Chapter 7: Triplets at the Theatre

1. dramatist- a person who writes plays
2. peruse- read something in a thorough and careful way
3. meticulous- very careful or precise
4. sprightly- lively and full of energy
5. restive- unable to stay still
6. mediaeval- relating to the Middle Ages
7. surreal- so awesome that it feels like a dream
8. to peter out- to gradually become smaller
9. silhouette- the dark shape or outline of someone
10. guffaw- a loud and hearty laugh
11. vantage- a place or position offering a good view of something
12. reprimand- to scold
13. jest- in a joking way

Chapter 8: The Triplets Go Shopping

1. potpourri- a mixture of things
2. hair-raising- extremely alarming or exciting
3. to be on one's last legs- very tired
4. scuttle- to run hurriedly with short quick steps
5. unabashed- not embarrassed, confused or ashamed
6. perennially- continuing for a long time, always
7. ingenious- clever, original or inventive
8. languid- showing no physical effort, in a leisurely manner
9. mystified- utterly bewildered
10. deja-vu- the feeling that you have already seen or experienced something, but is happening for the first time
11. faux- fake
12. salty- resentful or angry

Chapter 9: Mr Lion Goes to the Cinema

1. scintillating- sparkly or shining brightly
2. unwary- not cautious or aware of dangers or problems
3. spirited- full of energy, enthusiasm and determination
4. inquisitively- curiously
5. gobbledygook- nonsense
6. cock one's head- to tilt

7. lurk- to remain hidden as to wait in ambush for something or someone
8. lanky- tall and thin
9. grope- search blindly for something
10. burly- large and strong
11. despondently- feeling discouraged or depressed
12. lugubrious- looking or sounding sad or dismal
13. elaborate- detailed and complicated in design or planning
14. rhetorical- without expecting an explicit answer

Chapter 10: The Triplets Birthday

1. on an even keel- functioning normally after a period of difficulty
2. caboodle- a bunch of, or a collection of
3. numero dos- number two
4. ivories- teeth
5. salvage- rescue from a place
6. dictatorial- in a manner of total power
7. higgledy-piggledy- in confusion or disorder
8. ferret- to search for something
9. hue- shade of colour
10. swelter- uncomfortably hot
11. acrid- unpleasantly bitter
12. flail- wave or swing wildly
13. noble- having high moral principles